For Theo and Soli...

my magic mini monsters.

♡

Bloomsbury Publishing, London, Oxford, New York, New Delhi and Sydney

First published in Great Britain in 2017 by Bloomsbury Publishing Plc
50 Bedford Square, London WC1B 3DP

www.bloomsbury.com

BLOOMSBURY is a registered trademark of Bloomsbury Publishing Plc

Text and illustrations copyright © Sam Lloyd 2017

The moral rights of the author/illustrator have been asserted

A CIP catalogue record of this book is available from the British Library

ISBN 978 1 4088 6881 2 (HB)
SBN 978 1 4088 6882 9 (PB)
ISBN 978 1 4088 7388 5 (eBook)

All papers used by Bloomsbury Publishing are natural, recyclable products made
from wood grown in well managed forests. The manufacturing processes
conform to the environmental regulations of the country of origin

Printed in China by Leo Paper Products, Heshan, Guangdong

1 3 5 7 9 10 8 6 4 2

First Day at
Skeleton School

Sam Lloyd

BLOOMSBURY
LONDON OXFORD NEW YORK NEW DELHI SYDNEY

Deep, deep in this dark forest,
lurking amongst the trees,
there's a creepy night-time school
no human ever sees.

Listen . . . can you hear it?
There's a scary noise . . .

"Welcome," smiles Mr Bones.

"Meet the spooky girls and boys."

Skeleton School

It's their first day at Skeleton School,
they rattle, fly and float.
Let's go inside and look around . . .
Watch out for Monster Moat!

First it is assembly.
The spooks sing a creepy song.
"OWWWWWWW!" goes Walter Werewolf.
He loves to howl along.

But what do you learn at Skeleton School?
Shall we go and see?
Along a secret passageway...

. . . to the haunted library.

Wendy Witch is showing off –
the silly nincompoop!
Pussycat falls from her broom
when doing a loop-the-loop!

NO
daredevil stunts

Please leave
broomsticks
in here

Borrowing and returns

mice
are
nice

Spiffing
spells
for warty
witches

In dance class little skeletons
jingle-jangle to the beat.

Sonny Skeleton looks so cool
when he bops his bony feet.

At lunchtime zombies cook and serve
delicious things to eat:
snake sausages, beetle burgers
and pizza with mouldy meat.

Yippee! Now it's playtime.
Mr Bones zooms down the slide.
Bigfoot loves hide-and-seek —
but he finds it hard to hide!

Over in Cobweb Corner . . .
Look! There's Fred and Ted.
They're playing a game of throw and catch
with Frankie's big green head.

The ghosts learn how to float through walls whilst calling out "Whoo-ooooo!"

But Gary Ghost has had a bump.
He's not sure what to *doooooo*.

It's lucky that the nice school nurse
is an Egyptian Mummy,
she's got lots of bandages
around her big old tummy.

Frankie's in the sick room, too —
he's feeling a bit grotty.
He's in a funny muddle now
between his head and botty.

Poisonous Potions: do not touch!

Spider spit

Snake snot

Evil eyes

Bats' botty burps

Wizard Wilfred waves his wand ...
Crack! BANG! The cauldron flickers.
Good grief! Now Mr Bones has on ...

Skeleton School is over.
That's enough mischief for tonight!
"Be careful now" waves Mr Bones.
"Get home before daylight."

Listen . . . can you hear it?
There's a scary noise . . .

...On their way to

Human

School

are little girls
and boys!